# Keeper of the doves?

We heard noise behind the chapel. In silence Grand-mama led the way. At the back of the chapel she stopped, and so did we.

Mr. Tominski sat on a stump with his back to us. In the trees were doves, dozens of them. He called out something in a foreign language, and one of the doves flew toward him. Mr. Tominski held up a shiny object, and the dove took it in its beak and flew back to the tree.

Another foreign word. Another dove, until the trees were filled with doves holding these shiny pieces of metal.

Then there was one final cry and the doves flew to him. They circled his head, round and round, with the shiny objects glinting in the sunlight. Mr. Tominski threw back his head and cried with joy, "Hee! Hee! Hee!"

★ "[A] jewel-like novel . . . the snippets of Amie's and her family's lives add up to an exquisitely complete picture."
—*Publishers Weekly*, starred review

A KANSAS STATE READING CIRCLE BOOK

A PENNSYLVANIA SCHOOL LIBRARIANS ASSOCIATION
YOUNG ADULT TOP 40 NOMINEE

A RIVERBANK REVIEW CHILDREN'S
BOOKS OF DISTINCTION SHORT LIST TITLE

A DOROTHY CANFIELD FISHER AWARD
MASTER LIST SELECTION

PUFFIN BOOKS
Published by Penguin Group
Penguin Young Readers Group,
345 Hudson Street, New York, New York 10014, U.S.A.
Penguin Books Ltd, 80 Strand, London WC2R ORL, England
Penguin Books Australia Ltd, 250 Camberwell Road, Camberwell, Victoria 3124, Australia
Penguin Books Canada Ltd, 10 Alcorn Avenue, Toronto, Ontario, Canada M4V 3B2
Penguin Books (N.Z.) Ltd, 182-190 Wairau Road, Auckland 10, New Zealand

First published in the United States of America by Viking,
a division of Penguin Putnam Books for Young Readers, 2002
Published by Puffin Books, a division of Penguin Young Readers Group, 2004

5  7  9  10  8  6  4

THE LIBRARY OF CONGRESS HAS CATALOGED THE VIKING EDITION AS FOLLOWS:
Byars, Betsy Cromer.
The keeper of the doves / by Betsy Byars.
p.  cm.
Summary: In the late 1800s in Kentucky, Amen McBee and her four sisters both fear and
torment the reclusive and seemingly sinister Mr. Tominski, but their father continues to
provide for his needs.
ISBN: 0-670-03576-9 (hc)
[1. Sisters—Fiction.  2. Family life—Kentucky—Fiction.  3. Recluses—Fiction.
4. Kentucky—History—1865—Fiction.]  I. Title.
PZ7.B98396 Ke 2002    [Fic]—dc21    2002009283

Puffin Books ISBN 0-14-240063-7

Printed in the United States of America
Set in Wendy, Worcester
Book design by Teresa Kietlinski

# keeper

## of

## the

## doves

by Betsy Byars

PUFFIN BOOKS

# contents

# chapter one

# *A* for Amen

"Another girl? Not another girl? Don't tell me I've got another daughter!"

These were the first words my father spoke after I was born. Of course I was just minutes old—way too little to remember—but I have heard the story so often that I really think it is my memory.

It was a hot summer evening, 1891, and thunder could be heard as a storm rolled in from the west.

Papa's voice was very loud—especially when he was upset. The words certainly would have come through the door to Mama's room, rivaling the thunder for attention.

"She's a fine, healthy girl," Grandmama said. It was she who had brought the bad news. "Be grateful, Albert."

Papa seemed not to hear her. He looked up at the

1

ceiling. "What's left?" He dropped his hands to his sides in a gesture of hopelessness.

"We've got Abigail! Augusta! Arabella! Annabella!"

My father, in his despair, said the names so loudly that my sisters, thinking they had been summoned, rushed into the hall in their nightclothes.

"You have a sister," he said.

"A sister?" In my memory they were disappointed as well.

"Yes!"

"What's her name?" Abigail asked. As the oldest, she spoke for all of them.

"I'm thinking."

My father had insisted that his children's names all begin with an *A*. "When I have used up all the beautiful *A* names, I will move on to *B*," was his explanation.

"There's nothing left," he said.

"Does this mean you will go on to the *B*s?" Abigail asked.

I waited in my blanket for my fate. It came, but I was too little to know how I was doomed.

"Amen!" my father pronounced.

There was a silence.

"Papa, that's not a name," Abigail said, "That's something you say at the end of a prayer."

"It *is* the end of a prayer—a prayer for a son. Amen!"

"Albert," Grandmama said, "you're upset. Think about it and—"

"Amen!"

My father ran down the stairs. "Albert," Grandmama called after him, "the storm!" He slammed the screen door as he left the house, driven by his own inner storm.

In her room, my mother kissed my brow. She whispered, "We'll call you Amie," in a soothing way.

But in the family Bible—where it counts—it says: Born July 11, 1891, a daughter—Amen McBee.

# chapter two

# The Bellas and the Parts of a Dog

"Bellas! Bellas! Are you looking after your sister?"

"Yes, Aunt Pauline," the twins called back in unison.

"Well, don't get into any mischief."

"No, Aunt Pauline."

I had just had my third birthday and was, as usual, in the Bellas' care. The twins—Arabella and Annabella—were called the Bellas. No one—not even Mama—could tell them apart.

The Bellas were only two years older than I, but because there were two of them, they seemed twice as smart. They had taken me on as their personal improvement plan and on this day were enlarging my vocabulary.

We were beneath one of the willow trees from which our home got its name—The Willows. Keeping us company was Scout, the dog.

"What is that?" a Bella said, pointing to the dog.

"Chin."

"A dog doesn't have a chin," she said.

"He do."

"Do not."

"It be a little chin, but it do be a chin," I argued. My grammar wasn't perfect, but I did know the parts to a dog. I had recently learned that everything had a name and gobbled up words the way other three-year-olds gobble sweets.

Scout sat quietly, stoically waiting the outcome of the debate over his chin.

"Oh, all right. It *be* a chin," a Bella said, stressing my bad grammar.

Scout was Papa's dog, but he'd had four other little girls teach him patience, so he lay on his side, motionless except for his eyes, which rolled around, taking in everything. Without lifting his head, he could keep watch on the whole world.

I started over. "Chin . . . nose . . . eyebrow . . ."

I paused to glance from one twin to the other. Eyebrows, too, were sometimes disputed.

Neither twin answered. They were looking to the back of the house.

"Ear . . . neck . . . knee. . . . paw . . . toe . . . toenail."

I was just getting to "back," which always caused Scout's leg to jiggle with pleasure, when a low rumbling sound came from the dog.

I drew my hand back in alarm.

"He's growling at old man Tominski," a Bella said. "He doesn't like old man Tominski, and we don't either."

"I don't either," I said quickly, even though this was the first time I had ever heard the name.

"He spies on us."

"He wants to catch us, like that." The Bella's small hands curled into claws.

"Yes, like that."

Now the other Bella's hands formed identical weapons. With four hands reaching for me, I knew the first real fear of my life. I stepped back

"And let me tell you something," she said, as if she were Aunt Pauline, who was always stern with us.

"What?"

"When Scout growls, you better run."

"When Scout growls at somebody, there's something bad about that person."

"Something really, really bad."

I looked toward the barn, but there was no one there. "I don't see him," I said.

"You never see him, but he's there."

"Yes, he's there and he sees you!"

"But he's all gone," I said, hoping it was true.

"For now," the Bellas said in unison. They often spoke the same thought at the same time, as if their minds were connected.

Although I had not seen Mr. Tominski—and would not actually see him for several years—my dread of him had begun.

# chapter three

# Children!

"Children! Do not make faces behind my back!"

Aunt Pauline said this to the twins. I stood with my mouth open in amazement. How did Aunt Pauline see what they were doing? Our maid, Frances, had said, "That woman has eyes in the back of her head," but I had never been able to see them.

"Children, that's better." Aunt Pauline always said *children* as if the word itself was distasteful. Still she had not turned around.

Aunt Pauline was my father's sister who lived with us. She was officially in charge of the children. We had had nurses when we were infants, but as soon as we were considered girls, the kindly nurses disappeared and the unkindly Aunt Pauline took over.

On this day I had followed Aunt Pauline quickly from the dining room. At lunch she had made a comment about Mr. Tominski, and I wanted to ask her what she had said.

I had still never caught sight of the elusive Mr. Tominski, but he was always a dark shadow at the edge of my mind, just as he was at the edge of our lives.

I broke in with, "What did you say about Mr. Tominski, Aunt Pauline?"

"She said he was lurking around Frederick's memorial garden," a Bella said.

"What's 'lurking'?" I asked.

"Like this." The twins did a sinister turn around the room, hiding behind chairs and peering out.

This caused Aunt Pauline's frown to deepen. When she frowned, her nose got longer. Now it almost touched her lip.

"I also said that your father didn't need to visit the man every day and that Cook didn't need to take him meals."

She took a deep breath and went back to the original topic. "If you make ugly faces, children, your face will freeze like that."

With the sudden insight of a four-year-old, I said, "Is that what happened to your face, Aunt Pauline?"

There was a terrible silence, broken only by muffled laughter from the Bellas. I didn't see anything funny.

Now Aunt Pauline looked at me. There was such fury in her face that I stepped back. I would much rather she had looked at me with the eyes in the back of her head than the ones in the front.

"Children should be seen and not heard, Amen."

"Amen," the twins said in unison, as if they thought it was some sort of pronouncement.

"Children who ask questions will not learn the truth."

I knew that Aunt Pauline made up some of these things, but she looked as if she meant it, and then she swept from the room.

The twins collapsed on the love seat in laughter, kicking their feet in uncontrolled glee.

I was still awed by the terrible look from Aunt Pauline and wondering how you could learn the truth if you didn't ask questions. "What's so funny?" I asked.

The Bellas were good at imitating people. And as soon as Aunt Pauline was out of earshot one of the Bellas sat up and said, "Children!" It was Aunt

Pauline's voice. "Children, if you tell a lie, your nose will grow long and ugly."

The other Bella said in my voice, "Is that what happened to your nose, Aunt Pauline?"

They fell back again. More laughter, more kicking.

I was a serious child and was always surprised at the things others—particularly the Bellas—found funny.

Finally, their mirth spent, the Bellas went outside, and I followed. I tried to turn the conversation back to Mr. Tominski. "Why did Aunt Pauline say he was lurking in the memorial garden?"

The Bellas were busy making up a new Aunt Pauline insult and didn't answer.

"What does he do anyway?"

No answer.

"He must do something!" I was aware that all the people at The Willows had specific duties. That was how our food got prepared, our clothes laundered, our gardens tended.

"Somebody tell me what he does!" I remembered the Bellas had spotted him at the barn. "Is it something to do with the horses?"

But the Bellas' minds continued, trainlike, on a single track.

"Children, if you frown at a horse, your face will turn into one."

"Did you frown at a horse, Aunt Pauline?" Again, it was my innocent voice asking the question.

During the rest of the afternoon, in the middle of one of our games, one twin would break off and say, "Children," in that terrible Aunt Pauline way that made me wish I wasn't one of the group. "Children, if you say the word *witch*, you'll turn into one."

And my voice would pipe up from the other: "Did you say the word *witch*, Aunt Pauline?"

I still didn't see what was so funny, but by now, I had stopped asking for an explanation and made myself laugh along with them.

# chapter four

# A Daisy and Other Invisible Flowers

"Daisy ... dandelion ... daffodil ..."

My sister Augusta knew more words than anyone in the world. I loved to walk in the garden with her. It was like taking a walk with a dictionary.

Scout led the way. He paused and looked back occasionally to make sure we were following.

Augusta always started with aster and buttercup, and as she moved through the garden and the alphabet, she bent gracefully and picked imaginary flowers.

"Elderberry ... fuchsia ... gardenia." She added these to her bouquet.

It was a winter's day. The branches above us were bare. The only flowers were the invisible ones in my sister's arms.

We proceeded through the empty, colorless yard, with my sister going through the alphabet of flowers, gathering them one by one.

"...verbena...wisteria...the rare xanthenia—"
Here she paused to give me a wink of conspiracy.
Augusta was my serious sister, so even this sort of
mild joke was rare. She ended with "...yellow jas-
mine...zinnia."

Thus, we came to the family cemetery. This was
the end of the walk. I was always surprised at how
sad this made me, even though I had known it was
our destination.

"Open the gate for me, Amie."

She nodded at her flower-laden arms, and I
reached out for the latch.

The gate was black metal, an intricate design
with angels holding out harps to one another. Just
inside the gate was an ornate metal bench. Augusta
had told me on an earlier occasion that Aunt
Pauline always sat there before leaving the cemetery
so that if a ghost followed her, it would tire of waiting and return to its place.

My sister and I moved through the angels with
their harps, past the bench, to the graves. Scout
stayed behind with his tail drooping.

Most of the tombstones were old, some of the
names too weathered to read. But we moved to a

newer one where a tiny lamb looked down in sorrow at what lay beneath.

The inscription read

*Anita McBee*
*A Lamb of God*
*Born December 25, 1887*
*Departed this world January 3, 1888*

I always counted it on my fingers. "Ten days."

"Yes." My sister sighed.

"Do you remember Anita?"

"I will never forget. I got to hold her. She was the tiniest thing."

"I wish I had held her."

"You weren't born yet."

"I know, but still..."

"She was perfect—the tiniest fingers, fingernails. Her fingers curled around one of mine. I stroked the crown of her head—the softest hair. It was like corn silk. And she never cried—not one single time."

Augusta sighed. "Everything was perfect except her heart. The doctor listened to it and said she could only live a day or two. She surprised everyone by living for ten."

"Ten days." It seemed the saddest length of time—no time at all really, not enough to learn a single word.

"You know that song that Abigail and I sing—'Juanita'?" She sang the chorus. "Nita, Juanita, ask thy soul if we should part. Nita, Juanita, lean thou on my heart."

"I remember," I said.

"Well when I sing it, in my mind I'm singing, 'Nita, Anita, lean thou on my heart.' It brings tears to my eyes."

I knew that from now on it would bring tears to mine.

We stood in silence for a moment, and then Augusta opened her arms and her bouquet of invisible flowers rained down on our sister's tiny grave.

Sounds broke into our sorrow. A dove cooed. In the distance the noon train blew its mournful whistle.

Scout growled at the gate. The only other time I had heard him growl was when Mr. Tominski was near. I looked around quickly but saw nothing.

Augusta and I passed the bench without resting and joined the dog at the gate. The three of us walked in silence to the house.

# chapter five

# E Flat

"E! E! E!"

The twins were imitating Abigail and her singing teacher, Miss Printis. Miss Printis would occasionally tug the top of Abigail's hair and say "E—E—E" in order to get Abigail's voice up to the right note. Abigail did not have what Papa called "an ear for music."

The Bellas were using Scout as the reluctant singing pupil and tugging the top of his head.

"E! E! E!"

From the doorway Augusta said, "It's not nice to make fun of Abigail's singing. Anyway, quit tormenting the dog."

"He likes it, don't you, Scout. E! E! E!"

It was a rainy afternoon. Mama, Aunt Pauline, and Abigail had gone into town. Papa owned several businesses—McBee Bank, McBee Feed and Seed.

17

McBee Dry Goods was their destination today to buy material and trimmings for a dress for Abigail. Then they were off to the seamstress, so they would be gone a long time.

The Bellas and I were left at home, and we were hard up for something to do.

Augusta got tired of watching the dog's singing lesson. She said, "I'm going to play the piano. Do you want to come listen?"

"We'd rather teach Scout to sing, wouldn't we? E! E! E!"

"Amie, do you want to come? I'll play whatever you like."

Later I had reason to wish I had gone, but the attraction of the twins was strong. I shook my head.

Augusta went into the parlor and began to play the piano in a lively way, perhaps hoping to entice me into the room.

One of the Bellas said, "I know what we can play." Glancing at the doorway, she lowered her voice. "But we have to go upstairs so nobody can hear us."

The other Bella, reading her twin's mind, jumped up at once. I, not having that ability, was baffled.

"What is the game that we don't want anybody to hear?" I asked. The fact that it was something we didn't want anyone to hear should have warned me.

"Come on. You'll find out."

The twins moved into the hallway, and I followed.

Augusta stopped playing. "Where are you going?" she called.

"Nowhere," the Bellas called back.

"What are you going to do?"

"Nothing!"

"You're wearing what Aunt Pauline would call your up-to-no-good faces," Augusta sang out from the piano bench.

The three of us hurried upstairs to nowhere to do nothing.

# chapter six

# Fee Fi Fo Fum

"Fee Fi Fo Fum." The game was beginning.

One of the Bellas and I sat at the table where we had our lessons. The other Bella had disappeared into the hallway.

"When is the game going to start?" I had whispered again and again. "How will we know when the game starts?"

The Bella beside me had been twitching with excitement. "When the game starts, you'll know it!"

Now, apparently it had.

"Fee fi fo fum!" It came again, and this time the door was flung open. "I am old man Tominski and here I come! Be ye black! Be ye blue! You'll be both before I'm through!"

The Bella stomped into the room. She smiled, and her grin was terrifying. She had blacked out her front teeth with black paper, and the effect was so startling that for a moment I could not move.

Beside me, the Bella screamed and ran for the closet.

Now the heavy stomping feet were headed for me, the outstretched arms grasping for me.

"Run!" Bella cried at the closet door.

I jumped up so fast my chair fell to the floor. I ran, and Bella closed the door behind us.

The footsteps came closer and closer. In the closet we trembled. The footsteps stopped at the closet door. There was a silence, and then the door was flung open and the toothless Bella fell upon us with a roar.

I was genuinely afraid, but the Bellas laughed with success. "Let's do it again," the closet Bella said. "Only this time I get to be Mr. Tominski, all right? And you and Amie have to run from me. Only this time, Amie, run! You're supposed to run!"

"I will," I said.

"Give me the teeth."

Bella disappeared into the hall with her black paper, and the other Bella and I took our places at the table. We were pretending to read when we heard from the hallway, "Fee Fi Fo Fum! I'm old man Tominski and here I come!

"Be ye black! Be ye—"

She didn't get the second color out because a hand fell upon her shoulder. Papa stood in the doorway behind her.

For the first time I saw the resemblance between Papa and Aunt Pauline, because as his frown grew, so did his nose.

"What is going on here?"

"We were just playing," the Bella said, trying unsuccessfully to shrug off his hand.

"What's that on your teeth?"

"This? Oh, paper. I don't know how it got there."

"What were you doing?"

"Playing a game."

"I don't care for the game."

Silence.

"There's nothing funny or playful about making fun of a person."

"It was just old man—I mean, Mr. Tominski," the Bella beside me said.

"Mr. Tominski has been a member of this family longer than you have."

I was startled. I had never before thought of Mr. Tominski as a member of the family, but I said nothing.

"Not only has he been a member of this family, but he saved my life."

Now I could not keep quiet. "How, Papa?" I asked.

"I thought you knew the story."

"No, Papa."

"But you two did."

The Bellas didn't answer. Although the black paper had been removed from their teeth, it had left their front teeth gray.

He released the nearest Bella's shoulder. "Sit down, girls," he said. We sat at our table, as we did for lessons, and Papa stood in our tutor Mr. Trudeau's place.

"I was hunting by myself," Papa began. "My father had told me never to do that, but I had disobeyed. When I was climbing the Wilsons' fence, my gun went off and shot me in the shoulder.

"Mr. Tom was at the train tracks. He heard the gunshot, heard my yell, and found me. He picked me up and carried me in his arms three miles home.

"If Mr. Tom had not done that, I would have died." He looked at us, one by one. "You would never have been born." Another look. "All of us owe our lives to Mr. Tominski."

"I really didn't know that, Papa," I said.

"He laid me on the porch, beat on the door, hid until he saw the door open, and then ran. Later my father discovered he had taken refuge in the old chapel."

"That's why we don't go back there," one of the Bellas told me. "So we won't disturb him."

Papa nodded.

"The only thing my father ever asked of me was to look after Mr. Tom. I promised him on his deathbed that I would do that, and I intend to keep my promise. That's why I look in on him every day, why I make sure he's fed and clothed."

Papa's voice softened slightly as he said, "I am sure you and the twins will find another game, one that doesn't make fun of people I value."

"We will, Papa."

Papa gave us one final look, turned, and left the room. The three of us sat as if rooted in place.

Finally one of the Bellas said, "I still don't like him. He's not..."

She searched for the right word, couldn't find it, and borrowed a phrase of Aunt Pauline's. "He's not all there."

# chapter seven

# Grandmama

"Grandmama! I am the first to see Grandmama," I cried.

I had learned from the Bellas the importance of being the first, the last, the best, even the worst.

"You don't see Grandmama, you see the carriage," Augusta corrected.

My sisters and I stood on the front steps waiting to greet her. We wore pinafores of white dotted swiss over pale blue dresses of lawn. Dotted swiss... lawn... Even cloth has lovely names.

Mama was not going to come downstairs, so we had gone into her bedroom for approval. She had us turn around, and as our skirts swirled about us, she called us her white butterflies.

"I see the bird on her hat," I said. Grandmama was fond of big hats with colorful flowers and birds that looked ready for flight.

Papa was driving the carriage. He had gone into town to meet Grandmama, who arrived on the noon train. As he pulled up to the steps and stopped the horses, one of the Bellas said, "So where's this bird you saw?"

"Maybe it flew away," the other answered.

But I was too happy to see Grandmama to care about my mistake.

We went down the steps together, and starting with the oldest girl, Grandmama kissed us on our foreheads.

"Where's your mother?"

"She's upstairs," Abigail said. "I think she's resting at the moment."

"She needs her rest." Grandmama looked at Papa and then smiled at us. "Then I have time to take the girls' photographs. Albert, my camera is in my portmanteau." She pointed to a bag.

"Grandmama, you have a camera?" Augusta cried. "I didn't know ladies could take photographs."

"Nor I," my father replied.

"Nonsense, Albert," Grandmama said. "Ladies are far better at arranging photographs than men.

They have an eye for beauty and composition."

She took the camera from Papa. "This, girls, is a Kodak." It looked like a leather-covered box.

"It's small, Grandmama," Abigail said. We were accustomed to large cameras with men behind them hiding under a black cloth.

"It unfolds."

She opened it. One side sprang down, and the lens moved forward. Now it did look like a camera.

"Now I want you on the steps in the sunlight. Abigail, here. Augusta, here. No, move in a little closer, Augusta. Arabella and Annabella here. And you, Amen, will be in front, turned slightly sideways. Smooth your skirts over your legs, girls. Perfect."

She glanced at my father. "See, Albert, how easy it is for a woman to arrange an attractive photograph. Oh, I imagine when cameras were big heavy things, women never had a chance, but soon no woman will be without her camera."

She took several pictures of us on the stairs, then one of Papa sitting on a lawn chair with his pipe in his mouth and Scout at his feet. Although Papa had protested that he didn't want his photograph taken, he looked pleased about the whole thing, as did Scout.

"All dogs," Grandmama told us, "like to be photographed. And, girls, as a treat I have brought cameras for each of you, a Pocket Kodak so you can learn to take your own photographs."

"Can we have them now?" one of the Bellas asked.

At that moment Frances, Mama's maid, came out on the porch. "Mrs. Lily's awake now," she said.

"Ah, I'll go to her, but first, let me get a picture of you, Frances, over by the azaleas. Someday, I imagine, they will have cameras that will take pictures in color." She paused to take the picture and set the camera back in her bag.

As she went up the steps, she said, "Later, girls, I will give you your cameras and instruct you in how to use them."

She went into the house.

Grandmama's arrival, her energy, made it seem to me that The Willows had been like one of those castles in fairy tales with all the occupants sleeping their lives away. Now we were stirring, awakening to life.

It was months before I was to see the actual photographs Grandmama took that day, but then the photographs confirmed my feeling.

We were girls waiting for something to happen, girls whose lives were soon to be changed in a way we could not imagine.

# chapter eight

# The Telltale Hands

"Hands!" Grandmama tried to make her voice sound like Papa's.

We were at the dinner table, and Grandmama was relating one of her favorite stories about me.

"He made you and your sisters line up in front of his desk. On his desk was a sheet of paper stained with ink. Your papa's face was very stern." She made a stern face of her own.

"Hands!"

As she said the word a second time, I was back in Papa's study, holding out my hands. My sisters' hands were steady and clean. My own hands trembled and were stained with ink.

Papa looked at our hands and said, "Abigail, Augusta, Annabella, Arabella, you may go."

"Thank you, Papa," they chorused.

I could hear that they stopped just outside the

door to listen. "And close the door behind you," Papa said.

When the door closed, Papa looked at me. "What have you got to say for yourself?" Over his head was a portrait of his father wearing the same stern expression.

"I was trying..." I began but trailed off.

"Speak up! What were you trying to do? You know you are not allowed to touch anything on my desk. What was so important? What were you trying to do? Speak up!"

"I was trying to make a poem."

"A what?"

"A poem."

My father now looked puzzled, but over his head his father was still stern. "How old are you, Amen?"

"Six, Papa."

"Can you read?"

"Yes, Papa."

"Can you write?"

"Yes."

"What was the poem?"

"It wasn't very long."

"Good, there are enough long poems. Let's hear it."
I said my poem.
"Go on. What's the next line."
"That's the whole poem."
"It doesn't rhyme, Amen. A poem ought to rhyme." My father began to recite his favorite poem.

> *"He clasps the crag with crooked hands;*
> *Close to the sun in lonely lands,*
> *Ring'd with the azure world, he stands.*
> *The wrinkled sea beneath him crawls:*
> *He watches from his mountain walls,*
> *And like a thunderbolt he falls."*

"Tennyson was writing about an eagle."
"I know."
"That's my idea of a poem."
"Mine too."
He sighed. "Come here."
He took me on his lap. "Maybe a poem doesn't have to rhyme. I'm no expert." His long fingers gestured over his desk. "So you were trying to write down your poem."
"Yes, Papa."

"That makes sense. Would you like some help?"

"Yes, Papa."

Papa took a clean sheet of paper. He took my hand in his. We picked up the pen. We dipped the pen in ink. We wrote my poem.

*A poem is*
*a garden of words.*

"We'll put your name down at the bottom." We did that.

*Amen McBee*

Papa handed me the poem and took out his pocket watch. This was always his signal that the interview was over.

Grandmama's story was over too. She laughed in a kind way at the thought of my poem.

"How long ago was that, Amen? I lose track of time."

"Two years. I'm eight now."

"And do you still have the poem?"

"Yes."

"Well, you must show it to me. I'd like to see it. And do you remember what I called you?"

"I could never forget that, Grandmama. It was the nicest thing anyone ever said to me."

"What was it?" Augusta asked.

Grandmama said, "I called her my little word-smith. You know, like a goldsmith works with gold and a locksmith works with locks. My little word-smith."

# chapter nine

# I Shall Meet
# Thee Once More

*"I know I shall meet thee once more
Albeit at Heaven's great door."*

My sisters Abigail and Augusta were singing for Grandmama. It was Sunday evening. Normally we were not allowed to have music on Sunday, but Grandmama had begged for the rules to be relaxed, "just this once."

*"With a smile on my face
I'll accept thy embrace,
And we'll walk arm in arm as before."*

The Bellas and I sat on the horsehair sofa. I was trying not to slide off as I seemed to do on real horses.

This particular song had been written by and was at the request of Aunt Pauline. She stood behind the piano, her hand on a brooch at her neck. This pin contained the hair of a man Aunt Pauline had loved

35

and who had died during the war. A lock of his hair was twisted with a lock of hers, and it was all she had left of Frederick.

Augusta had told me that while Frederick had died "during the war," he had died of chicken pox. I was never, never to mention this, especially not to the twins, who would probably cackle like chickens every time his name was mentioned.

My sisters started on the chorus.

> *"Once more, just once more*
> *May we meet on that heavenly shore.*
> *Once more, just once more*
> *May we walk arm in arm as before."*

One of the Bellas was amusing the other by tugging the top of her hair and mouthing, "E—E—E."

Suddenly the Bellas gasped. They did this exactly together, and I looked from one to the other. Their eyes were turned to the window, and I saw it.

A terrible face was there, grinning. The front teeth were missing, and the eyes beneath low, dark brows had an animal shine.

Instantly I was back in the classroom and I wanted to run and hide in the closet. I could not do this, of course—the parlor had no closet—but I began to whimper with fear.

Aunt Pauline gave me one of her worst frowns. Her nose touched her upper lip. She was the only one allowed to show emotion during "In Memory of Frederick."

My singing sisters, seemingly unaware of the frightful face at the window, sang the final "May we walk arm in arm as before."

Aunt Pauline's fingers tightened on her brooch. She sighed.

I looked back at the window. The face was gone, but it was branded on my mind, the way the image of the sun lingers on the eye. My heart pounded in my chest.

Grandmama said, "Could we have something a little more cheerful, girls?"

Abigail said, "This is from *The Mikado*, Grandmama. It's supposed to be 'Three Little Maids from School,' but Miss Printis lets us say 'Two Little Maids' because that's all we are. Is that all right with you, Grandmama?"

"Indeed! I like children who can adapt."

Abigail struck a chord on the piano.

*"Two little maids from school are we.*
*Pert as a schoolgirl well can be.*
*Filled to the brim with girlish glee.*
*Two little maids from school."*

Augusta was busy playing the piano, but Abigail was snapping her imaginary fan like a Japanese lady.

I only half watched my sisters. My other half was concentrated on the window.

When, at last, the singing was over, the Bellas and I left the room. I trailed after them—still tormented by the face at the window.

"Anyway," one of them was saying, "if Frederick and Aunt Pauline do meet on that heavenly shore, he's going to run for his life. He's going to be young and handsome and she's going to be old and ugly, isn't that right?"

"Right," said the other Bella.

I did not mention that he might be slightly disfigured with chicken pox and therefore glad to see anybody—even an elderly Aunt Pauline.

I touched the backs of the Bellas' pinafores with trembling hands.

"Was that him?" I said, my voice trembling too.

"Who?"

"You know. Mr. Tominski?"

"Of course. Who'd you think it was? Santa Claus?"

"What happened to his teeth?"

"He broke them off eating children."

I gulped with shock. "That's not true."

"Yes, it is!" they said together. They never contradicted each other.

"I don't believe it."

"Well, it's true."

"Even if he saved Papa's life, Papa wouldn't let him stay if he did that. He wouldn't let Cook take him his meals. He wouldn't—"

"Don't believe us then. We don't care."

"That's right. We don't care. If you don't believe us, just go walking back in the woods. You'll find out."

I had never been drawn to the woods the way the twins seemed to be. I would often stop at the edge, watch them disappear and return to the house.

That night I dreamed of the toothless face. In my dream, Mr. Tominski looked at me. Blood dripped from his mouth. He licked his lips and grinned.

I woke up trembling.

# chapter ten

# Jekyll, Hyde, Abigail, and I

"*Jekyll and Hyde.*"

Abigail turned the book so I could read the whole title. *The Strange Case of Dr. Jekyll and Mr. Hyde*, by Robert Louis Stevenson.

I recognized it as one of Papa's books—the brown leather binding, the gold letters. Papa was very particular about his books.

"Did Papa say you could read that outside?"

"I didn't ask. He would just try to get me to read something more appropriate like *Treasure Island*."

"Why isn't this book appropriate? What's it about?"

"It's about a man with two personalities, and one of them is good and the other one is eeeee-vil." She smiled.

"Read me a little bit."

I climbed into the hammock beside her. Abigail

always smelled of spices, because she kept little bags of cinnamon and cloves stuck in with her petticoats.

Abigail was our beautiful sister. Her hair was curlier, her eyelashes thicker, her cheeks rosier. She was exactly like a painting of Mama when she was a girl.

In the hammock our faces were close together, and I could see the tiny dimples in the corners of her mouth.

Abigail opened the book to the first page.

"Now, this is a description of a person's face. Who does it sound like?"

Abigail read, "'—was never lighted by a smile; cold, scanty ... lean, long, dusty, dreary ...'"

"I don't know."

"Give up?"

"Yes."

"Aunt Pauline. Doesn't that perfectly describe Aunt Pauline? Cold, scanty, long, dusty, dreary. Except for the last of the sentence, 'and yet somehow lovable.'"

She laughed, trying to look wicked. "I'm part evil, like the man in the book."

"No, you aren't," I said. No one could look wicked with dimples in the corners of her mouth. "It's true about Aunt Pauline. Her face does look like that."

One of the things that united us, that made us feel closer as sisters, was a mutual dislike of Aunt Pauline.

"Later on in the book," Abigail continued, beginning to turn the pages, "these two friends of his are outside Dr. Jekyll's house—Jekyll is the good one. Hyde's the evil one. And they're talking to him. Dr. Jekyll is just a face in the window—and slowly he starts to turn into Mr. Hyde. Let me see if I can find the place." She found it and read dramatically.

> *"But the words were hardly uttered before the smile was struck out of his face and succeeded by an expression of such abject terror and despair, as froze the very blood of the two gentlemen below. They saw it but for a glimpse, for the window was instantly thrust down; but that glimpse had been sufficient...."*

She said, "You know what that reminds me of—a face in the window that 'froze the very blood'?"

"Mr. Tominski," I whispered.

"Yes. I saw him watching us sing the other night, did you?"

"Yes. The Bellas told me he eats little children. I said I didn't believe it, but that night I had a bad dream, and in the dream he did eat one, and then he turned and looked at me and he gave me a 'you're next' look and I tried to run but my legs wouldn't work and I woke up—"

Abigail hushed me by touching a finger to her lips. I glanced around quickly, afraid she had seen Mr. Tominski, but the yard was empty.

"What?"

"Mama and Grandmama," she said. "I want to hear what they're saying."

She leaned across me to get a better view of the porch. I inhaled the scent of cinnamon and clove.

"Grandmama has only been here one week," she reminded me, "and I've already heard her and Mama argue at least three times."

This was news to me. "What do they argue about?"

"Oh, this and that. They even had one argument about you."

"Me?" My body stiffened. The thought made me uneasy. "What? What? Tell me!"

"Oh, Grandmama thinks the Bellas are not a good influence. She thinks you are a very bright girl—you must have showed her some of your poems."

"She asked to see them."

"Well, she expected to see two or three, and you had how many?"

"Thirty, maybe forty. Was that too many? What else did she say?"

"She said the constant influence of the Bellas was bound to—how did Grandmama put it?—'dull even a budding genius.' Then Mama said that perhaps, if you were a budding genius, you could raise the Bellas' level of intelligence."

"Budding genius? They said that?" I added, "Then what?" although I really didn't want to hear any more.

Abigail's voice took on a tone of conspiracy. "Let's go see what this argument is about, want to? Maybe it's about me."

She marked her place in the book with a red satin ribbon and climbed out of the hammock. "Come on," she said.

I lay there, unable to move.

"Come on! They might be talking about *you*!"

At that, I managed to stumble out of the hammock, landing on my knees. Abigail helped me to my feet and put her arm through mine. Then, just two sisters enjoying the afternoon, we made our way to the porch.

# chapter eleven

# Keeper of the Doves

"Keeper of the doves?"

"Mother, please lower your voice. I am not deaf."

"But a dove keeper?" If anything, Grandmama's voice got louder. "You never mentioned that before. What does a keeper of the doves do?"

Unnoticed by Grandmama or Mama, Abigail and I sat down on the steps. Abigail glanced at me and mouthed the word *Tominski*. But I had already sensed the conversation was about him and found myself relieved it was not about me.

"Nobody needs a dove keeper!"

"Mother, please."

"If the man's got to keep something, why not bees? At least you would get honey out of that."

"Mother, I don't want Albert to hear this."

"Albert's gone to the lumber mill with the Bellas. That's why it's so quiet around here."

"I wouldn't say it was quiet, Mother."

"Well, I'd really like to know what the man actually does."

I had wondered that most of my life.

"Mr. Tominski is a harmless old man, Mother. The connection goes back to Albert's childhood. He's part of family history."

"Albert, like Pauline, dwells too much in the past. They should—"

"I know, Mother, turn their faces to the future." Mama spoke as if she had heard this phrase many, many times.

"But what does he do? Answer me that. Everyone should do something, even a harmless old man—if indeed he is harmless."

"Mother!"

"Well, I've never laid eyes on the man. How can I judge whether he's harmless or not."

She took a deep breath and slapped her hands on the arms of her rocker. Plainly a decision had been made.

"And I think it's high time I saw the man and his famous doves."

Grandmama turned and noticed us for the first time.

"Girls!"

"Yes, Grandmama," we said. For once Abigail and I were as in unison as the Bellas.

"Do you know where these famous doves are?"

"Yes, Grandmama," Abigail said. "The cages are at the old chapel."

"He keeps doves in the chapel?" Grandmama made it sound like blasphemy.

"Behind the chapel, Mother."

"Still..." Grandmama stood. "Take me there!" she ordered.

"Albert doesn't like for the children to bother the doves."

"Children bother doves?" Grandmama made it sound like the most ridiculous thing in the world. "Come, girls."

Grandmama swept down the stairs and took the pebbled path through the roses. We followed.

I, still troubled by my nightmare, came more slowly. I glanced back at my mother. The setting sun cast its final rays on her face, and she lifted her hand and touched her forehead, as she sometimes did to ward off a headache.

We skirted the orchard—Rome apples, Bosc pears—and then moved past the kitchen garden. Past the herb garden, the names of the herbs as lovely as their scents—rosemary, tansy, caraway, thyme. For once Abigail did not pause to crush a few leaves and rub the scent on her arms.

We continued. Not being one to explore, I had never ventured beyond the gardens before.

As we moved along the small overgrown path, I seemed to remember the Bellas had warned me about the woods, but except for the fact that Mr. Tominski lived here, I could remember no details. Still, the air seemed to have thickened around me.

The chapel took me unawares. It was a wooden building, quite small. The door stood open, and inside we could see a potbelly stove and furniture that seemed to have been made from pews.

We heard noise behind the chapel. In silence Grandmama led the way. At the back of the chapel she stopped, and so did we.

Mr. Tominski sat on a stump with his back to us.

In the trees were doves, dozens of them. He called out something in a foreign language, or maybe it was a familiar word made foreign by lack of teeth.

One of the doves flew toward him. Mr. Tominski held up a shiny object, and the dove took it in its beak and flew back to the tree.

Another foreign word. Another dove.

Finally the trees were filled with doves holding these shiny pieces of metal.

Then there was one final cry and the doves flew to him. They circled his head, round and round, with the shiny objects glinting in the sunlight. Mr. Tominski threw back his head and cried with joy, "Hee! Hee! Hee!"

Grandmama noticed something on the ground, bent to pick it up, and with an abrupt tug on our shoulders, turned us around. We walked quietly around the chapel.

When we were out of earshot, Grandmama said, "Well, I am at a loss for words."

Then she disproved the statement by continuing immediately with, "Those were pennies, see?"

"Pennies?"

She held one of the pennies in the palm of her

hand. "The man flattened copper pennies on the railroad track, drilled a tiny hole in them, and strung them up like ornaments.

"That was quite something, girls. And I think—remind me to ask Albert, I don't dare bring up the subject again with Lily—I think he was speaking Polish."

She continued to the porch. "Though I think your papa was right. You should stay away from the chapel."

"I will," I promised.

As we climbed the stairs, we saw that Mama had gone into the house.

Grandmama sat in one of the rockers. "I'd like to take a photograph of that man," she said. She leaned back and set her rocker in motion. Grandmama could always put a flattering light on someone when she wished.

Just as she had called me a wordsmith, now she said of Mr. Tominski, "The man is a dove magician."

# chapter twelve

# Leaving

*Leave an* i *out of* said,
*I get sad.*
*Leave an* e *off of* made,
*I get mad.*

This was my new poem. I had been working on it all morning. I couldn't wait to finish so that I could show it to Papa. He would like it because it rhymed. Also it was about words, and I knew Papa loved words too—almost as much as I did.

Just the other evening he had looked up from his book, as he occasionally did, and said, "Here's a word for you, Amen."

"What is it, Papa?"

"*Lambency.*"

Aunt Pauline had jabbed her needle into her embroidery frame and left it there. "Is that a disease, Albert?"

"No, Pauline, no. This is Henry James. Henry James isn't interested in disease."

In the silence I repeated the word, *"lambency,"* enjoying the sound. "How is it used, Papa?"

He read the phrase—"'a strange mocking lambency which must have been part of her adventurous youth.'"

"I give up, Papa."

"It's a kind of glow, I believe, a radiance."

*"Lambency.* I'll remember that, Papa." I enjoyed getting a new word, even one that would be difficult to use.

I went back to my poem. In the second part, I would put a letter into a word. I had already composed the first two lines in my mind.

> *Put an* o *into* bat,
> *You get* boat.
> *Put an* o *into* flat,
> *It will* float.

Papa had put a special table in the corner of our schoolroom so that I would have a place to write my poems. I was sitting there, copying the lines onto the paper, when the Bellas came in.

"What are you doing?" one of them asked.

"She's doing her po-ems," the other Bella said scornfully.

"You'll enjoy this one," I said. "It's funny. See, I figured out that if you take a letter out of a word, you get another word, like—"

The Bellas didn't wait to hear. "Mama wants to see you."

"Why?"

"We aren't allowed to tell you, are we?"

"No, we aren't allowed to tell you."

The way they said this alarmed me.

"Have I done something wrong?"

"We aren't allowed to tell you!" they said together.

"But—"

"We aren't allowed to tell you. All we can tell you is that Mama wants to see you."

"Where is she?"

"Where she always is—in her room."

My alarm blossomed. I could not remember the last time I had been summoned to Mama's room by myself.

I glanced down at my unfinished poem. "Do you suppose Mama would like to see my poem?"

"She doesn't want to see your stupid po-em, she wants to see you."

"And we aren't allowed to tell you why."

"No, we aren't allowed to tell you why."

Leaving my poem on the writing desk, I walked out of the room and down the hall to Mama's room. There were eight rooms on this floor, and Mama's was at the end.

My steps slowed as I went over the events of the past week.

The only thing I could think of that might have distressed Mama was Abigail and me going to the chapel where Mr. Tominski kept his doves.

I had not seen Mama since that afternoon on the porch. My last glimpse of her had been as she lifted her hand to touch her forehead.

Had Abigail and I caused her pain? Was Abigail being summoned too? I took some comfort in the thought of standing with my sister.

The door to Mama's room was open. Crossing my fingers for luck, I stepped inside.

# chapter thirteen

# In Mama's Room

Mama sat at her dressing table. I watched from the doorway. Mama's room was like a garden. Flowers were printed on a fabric called chintz, and the colors were natural colors that you saw in the garden—rose and lilac.

Mama held a bottle of scent in one hand and with the other she touched the bottle's stopper behind her ear.

I was reluctant to go any farther without permission.

"I wish I smelled good," I said.

Mama smiled at me in the mirror and beckoned me over. She touched the glass stopper behind each of my ears. It was cool and smelled so good I wanted it to last forever.

"Lily of the valley," Mama said, knowing I liked to know the name of everything.

"A perfume named for you, Mama."

"That's why your papa bought it. He said, 'I wish it were Lily of The Willows.'" It must have been a happy memory, for she smiled.

The top of Mama's dressing table was rose marble, and on it were cut-glass bottles of scent and silver boxes that held combs and fine face powder. There was a beautiful silver comb and brush set.

Now I noticed that new to the table were small boxes of pills and brown bottles of medicine. I knew that summers were difficult for Mama because of allergies that I did not understand. Sometimes it seemed I had two mothers, a reclusive summer one and a bright and spirited winter one. Still, I had never seen so many medicines.

My apprehension about myself and what I had done wrong now turned to concern for Mama.

"Mama, are you ill?"

A feeling of guilt came over me for thinking only of myself. The Bellas were right when they said my poems were stupid.

"Mama, what's wrong?" At this point I actually hoped I had done something wrong. Anything would have been better than for Mama to be ill.

Mama's smile softened. She took my hand and laid it on her stomach. I noticed with dismay that, as usual, I had ink stains on my fingers.

Then I felt something move. I tried to draw back my hand, but Mama covered my hand with hers.

"What is that?" I asked.

"That is your little brother or sister," Mama said.

"A baby?"

"Yes."

"You're going to have a baby?"

"Yes."

"When?"

"It's going to be soon now. That's why Grandmama's here. She's been here to welcome each of you into the world."

"How soon?"

"A week or two. Maybe sooner."

"How can you tell?"

"Well, Amie, this will be my seventh baby, so I know what to expect. I'm counting on all of you girls to help me."

"Have the baby?"

"No, no, I have plenty of that kind of help. I just need for you girls to be kind to one another and to

Grandmama. Do what Aunt Pauline tells you. I'll be busy looking after the baby. You'll understand that, won't you?"

"Yes."

Mama moved her hand, and I took mine back and put it in the pocket of my apron.

"I'll be good, Mama. I promise."

"Thank you, Amie. I knew I could count on you."

Just as Papa took out his pocket watch to signal our dismissal, Mama touched her fingers on the dressing table, as if she were playing one light, quick chord on the piano.

"I'm glad about the baby, Mama."

"I am too, Amie."

I walked back to the room in a sort of daze. "We know, we know," the Bellas said together. "Mama's going to have a baby. Mama's going to have a baby. We knew that months ago."

"I didn't."

"Didn't you notice how fat she was getting?"

"No."

"The baby's in her stomach."

"I know. She let me feel it move."

"She didn't let us, but we didn't want to, did we?"

"No, we didn't want to."

"You stink," a Bella said.

"Mama put some perfume on me."

"She didn't put any on us, did she?"

"No, we didn't want any on us."

"We didn't want to stink."

I waited out the conversation and then said, "Why does Mama have to take all that medicine?"

"So it will be a boy!" one of the Bellas said. The other Bella gave her twin a quick look of admiration for the creative reply.

She added, "You don't think she wants another girl, do you?"

"Papa doesn't. You should have heard him yell his head off when you were born."

One of the Bellas became my father bellowing out, "Another girl? Not another girl!"

Her imitation of Papa's dismay was good enough to hurt me. I had heard the story many times before, and I had gotten used to the hurt, but seeing it dramatized made me unhappy all over again.

"I just hope the baby will be all right," I said.

# chapter fourteen

# The Nevers

"Never open an umbrella in the house."

"Never sleep with the full moon on your face."

"Break a mirror, you have seven years' bad luck."

Those were some of Aunt Pauline's rules. She had a deep respect for bad luck and its prevention. She seemed to see life as a narrow and dangerous cliff, with charmed objects and correct action all there was to keep you from falling over the edge.

She made us throw salt over our left shoulders if we spilled some. She made us turn around three times if a hearse passed by. She made us promise never to look in a mirror at bedtime or the devil would come into our dreams.

"Never, never tell a bad dream before breakfast or it will come true."

That was one of her favorite rules—I had been

hearing it all my life. Now it was she herself who broke that rule.

She came into the kitchen where we girls were having breakfast at the table. The cook, Rose, was cutting us slices of bread. Aunt Pauline leaned heavily against the table.

"You all right, Miss Pauline?" Cook asked. We looked at our aunt. She did look a bit worse than usual.

Aunt Pauline put one hand to her throat, as if seeking the comfort of her brooch containing Frederick's hair, but in her agitation, she had forgotten to pin it on that morning.

She hesitated, took a deep breath, and then blurted out, "I dreamed I was in a graveyard."

Cook's knife stopped in the middle of a slice. The bread and the knife dropped to the table.

"What does that mean, Aunt Pauline?" Abigail asked.

Aunt Pauline shook her head as if she couldn't bring herself to say the words.

"It means that someone's going to die," Cook said in a hushed tone. Cook shared Aunt Pauline's belief in dreams and superstitions. A broom rested by the back door to prevent a spell from entering. Willow twigs by the window kept out the evil eye.

"Who's going to die?" a Bella asked.

"Could you see the name on the tombstone, Miss Pauline?" Cook asked.

"I never can," Aunt Pauline said. "I've had this dream before. It's always the same. I come in the graveyard and I start running. I'm terribly afraid. I run and I run, but I don't seem to be getting anywhere."

We had stopped eating, caught up in the nightmare. For once Aunt Pauline had our complete attention.

"Finally I get to the empty grave and just as I lift my eyes to read the name, I wake up shivering."

"I don't believe in that kind of thing," Abigail said.

"It doesn't matter whether you believe or not," Cook said. "It always comes true."

"It won't be one of us, will it?" I asked.

"Yes, Miss Pauline," Cook said, "had the grave been dug for an adult or a child?"

I drew in my breath. I remembered that Mama was going to have a baby. I remembered the tiny grave in our cemetery. I remembered how fragile a baby's heart was.

Aunt Pauline put out her hands as if to part a curtain.

"I couldn't see," she said. "In the dream, there is always a lot of fog. As I run, I stumble again and again." She looked through the fog, her sharp eyes turning from stove to table, but the size of the grave was not there.

Papa appeared in the doorway. "Are you ill, Pauline?"

"Albert, I dreamed of a graveyard," she said, turning.

Papa's face hardened. "Whatever you do, Pauline, don't bother Lily with your voodoo and mumbo jumbo."

"But, Albert," Aunt Pauline began, "she would want to know. She asked me if I had dreamed whether the baby would be a boy or a girl. If there is trouble ahead, she would want to prepare." Plainly Mama had been next on her list.

"I mean what I say. I don't want Lily upset. She's very fragile right now."

Aunt Pauline didn't respond.

Cook said, "He's right, Miss Pauline. We need to keep this to ourselves. Miss Lily needs her peace."

"I won't tell," Aunt Pauline conceded. "I didn't want to tell in the first place. I came in the kitchen and everyone could see I was upset and asked what was wrong...." She trailed off.

"We won't tell either," Abigail said. "We don't believe in mumbo jumbo."

"I wasn't worried about you girls," Papa said.

After Papa left the room, Augusta said, "Aunt Pauline, you know what's going to happen now. You told the bad dream before breakfast."

"Yes," the Bellas said in unison, "now it's going to come true."

# chapter fifteen

# Once upon a Time

"Once upon a time..."

My sister Abigail had started a story. It was hard to be interested. Mama was having her baby.

The five of us had been sent to bed early. We were in our nightgowns, as Grandmama had instructed. "This may take a long time," she had warned us.

It was now seven o'clock in the evening. For two hours we had been sitting on the big bed Abigail and Augusta shared.

Although my sisters had been through this before, I had not. The visions that flitted through my mind like moths were troubling ones—Aunt Pauline's dream of the graveyard that she had told before breakfast, the little stone lamb in our cemetery, the bottles of medicine and pills Mama was taking.

The Bellas seemed untroubled by moths. One of them asked for the second time, "Did we have any supper?"

"I don't think we did. Let's go to the kitchen."

"Grandmama told us to stay in our room and not come out till she called us, and yes, we did have supper."

Abigail, sensing she did not have our attention, started over.

"Once upon a time there were five sisters."

"I don't like stories about us," one of the Bellas said. "I like stories about giants and wicked witches and dragons that eat people."

"Each sister," Abigail continued, "was known for a particular trait."

She made a point of glancing at herself in the mirror. She must have been pleased by her image, for she smiled. She had once said that the difference in people was that some of them smiled when they looked in the mirror, and the others didn't.

"The older sister had beauty."

"She means herself," one of the Bellas said scornfully.

Augusta, smiling, said teasingly, "And was the

beautiful older sister in love with the prince of a neighboring land?"

Abigail blushed, and she did look beautiful in her pink nightdress, pink ribbons in her hair, pink roses on her slippers.

She paused to see if there were any more interruptions, and then went on with her story.

"One sister could play the piano like an angel."

"That's supposed to be you, Augusta."

"One sister knew all the words in the world."

"I wish I did," I said, beginning to enjoy the story.

"And two of the sisters were imps."

"Imps! Imps! We don't want to be imps!" The Bellas cried this in perfect unison. To this day, I don't know how they managed it.

"Let me finish. The imps had special power."

"What kind of power?"

"If you would quit interrupting, I could tell you."

"Make it that we had the power to become invisible."

"Yes, if we were invisible we could leave this room and go downstairs and get something to eat."

"Yes, and then we could walk into Mama's room and see what's happening."

"The imps had the power to . . ." Abigail paused for emphasis.

At that moment, the door opened abruptly and Grandmama stood there, beaming.

"Girls," she said, "your new baby brother has arrived."

"A brother?" Abigail asked.

"Yes. You can see him now, but just for a minute."

We followed her down the hall to Mama's room, as usual in the order of our births. On the way, we passed our father. He was sitting in a hall chair, his face in his hands. He was weeping.

I had never seen any sign of weakness in my father before, and to see him in tears was upsetting.

I thought of Anita's fragile heart and stumbled on the carpet. "Is there something wrong with the baby?" I asked.

Grandmama, hearing my concern, beamed over her shoulder. "Tears of joy, my dears, tears of joy."

One of the Bellas asked Grandmama's back, "Did he cry when we were born?"

"Yes," the other Bella said, "but those were not tears of joy."

We went single file into Mama's room. Mama was

in bed, propped up on pillows. Her golden hair fanned out on either side of her face.

The baby lay in the crook of her arm. Mama watched the small wrinkled face with a proud smile.

"This is your brother," she said.

We hesitated. My sisters probably felt as I did—out of place—the five sisters from the fairy tale who find themselves at the ball in their nightclothes.

It was Abigail who managed to speak for all of us. "He's very nice, Mama," she said.

"Out! Out!" Grandmama said. "Your mother and brother need their rest."

We went without any more coaxing. I, for one, was not sorry to go.

chapter sixteen

# Passing the Baby

"Please pass the baby," Augusta said.

"My five minutes aren't up yet," Abigail said. "You are the most beautiful baby in the world. Yes, you are. You—"

Papa was holding his pocket watch in one hand. He glanced at it.

My sisters and I were lined up on the sofa to hold our new baby brother. Abigail was first because she was the oldest.

"Papa, it's got to be my turn now," Augusta said. "Please pass the baby."

Grandmama was standing beside Papa, concerned that the transfer go smoothly. Her arms were half raised to assist if needed.

"It's time," Papa said.

Grandmama moved forward quickly. "Now be careful of his head." She lifted Adam and laid him across Augusta's lap, his head cradled on her arm. I could see a spot on the top of his head where something pulsed.

Then it was Arabella's turn. Then Annabella's. Their turn was a bit shorter, because after about two minutes, the first Bella said, "You can have him now." The second Bella started to fidget even sooner.

"Please pass the baby, if you're through," I said, smoothing my skirt over my knees. I wished my lap wasn't so thin, because I didn't want my brother's first impression of me to be one of discomfort.

Grandmama laid Adam on my lap. I looked down at my brother and a wave of love washed over me. Up until this moment, his birth had been only a major upset in my life, and so I was unprepared for the strength of my emotion.

"Time," Papa said. He returned his pocket watch to its pocket.

"Already? I just got him," I said.

"It was five minutes, Amie," Grandmama said firmly. "Now Adam needs to go up to his mother. Nurse!"

The nurse had been standing in the doorway, and she came forward quickly. Grandmama took Adam from me and held him for a moment before passing him to the nurse. My lap seemed suddenly empty.

"Adam is lucky to have such nice, polite, and loving sisters, aren't you, Adam?" Grandmama said. "Aren't you a lucky little boy?"

"And we're lucky to have him," Abigail said.

"Amen," said Papa.

I looked up but I knew he was not calling my name.

That afternoon I wrote:

> *Five minutes I held my brother.*
> *I could have held him all day.*
> *But Papa's watch said time was up*
> *And Grandmama took him away.*

Of course the poem didn't make it as wonderful as it was. That's the only trouble with words. There are thousands and thousands of them, but sometimes you cannot find the one you need.

At any rate that was one of the happiest mornings of my life. My brother really did seem to have banished unhappiness from The Willows. It was like something from one of Abigail's fairy stories.

I thought I would never know sorrow again. But, as it turned out, I was wrong.

# chapter seventeen

# Quick. Hold That Pose.

"Quickly now," Grandmama said.

We were approaching our new brother with our Pocket Kodak cameras, which Grandmama had, at last, presented.

Grandmama's instructions had been hurried. "You have twelve exposures. This is your viewfinder. You look through it and when you see a picture you want to take, you press the shutter, here."

The Bellas had rashly already taken a few pictures of each other making faces before the instructions, and so they only had eight exposures left. Abigail, Augusta, and I had each taken one picture of Scout and so had eleven exposures remaining.

"The pictures will be small," Grandmama said, "just about so big, so you have to plan carefully."

"We will," I cried with enough enthusiasm for all of us.

"And keep the sun behind you."

"We will!"

The camera in my hand, small as it was, gave me a feeling of power. It was the way pen and paper made me feel. Creating something is the headiest feeling in the world.

Adam was on Mama's lap. "Now, don't get me in the picture," Mama said.

"Nonsense, Lily," Grandmama said, "you look quite nice. Let the children take what they will."

The morning passed quickly. After lunch the Bellas, cameras in hand, went with Papa to look at a litter of spaniel puppies at the Wilsons. Augusta, Mama's shadow these days, was upstairs rocking the baby. Abigail was in the front yard with her beau, Lamar.

Lamar and Abigail were taking pictures of each other. I heard Lamar say, "Abigail, you must promise me something."

"What's that, Lamar?"

"Promise me first."

"Why, Lamar, you rascal. I never promise before I know what the promise is."

"You must promise to give me one of the photographs."

"A photograph of yourself. Why, how vain you are, Lamar."

"Not of me, of you, Abigail."

"You want a picture of me in this old housedress? Never!" The dress was new and Abigail looked, as usual, beautiful.

"I'll think about it, Lamar. By the time they are developed, you'll have forgotten all about me."

While Lamar continued to plead, I went around the house, looking for things to photograph.

In early afternoon things seemed to stop around here. I had once tried to write a poem about it.

> *Nap time at The Willows.*
> *Heads upon our pillows.*
> *The noon train has come and gone.*
> *The whole world, with us, slumbers on.*

I paused at the cemetery. Over the fence, I could see the stone lamb of Anita's grave.

My grip on the Kodak tightened. I would take a picture of the lamb.

I opened the gate. As usual, it creaked on its hinges.

I moved toward the lamb. For a moment I just

stood there. My thoughts were of Anita and how glad I was that there would not be another small grave beside this one.

Just then, a butterfly landed on the stone lamb. I held my breath. I looked through the viewfinder. There it was.

The butterfly flexed its wings, once, again. My fingers fumbled for the shutter. I inched toward the grave and sank to my knees.

I heard the gate open behind me. I thought it was probably Aunt Pauline. Ever since the photography had begun, she had been posing here and there— leaning against a porch column, smelling a flower in Frederick's memorial garden, gazing off into the distance.

If I got this photograph, I decided, I would be generous and take one of Aunt Pauline.

There. One click and it was done. I turned to Aunt Pauline, smiling with satisfaction.

It was not Aunt Pauline, however, who smiled back at me. It was Mr. Tominski.

His gap-toothed grin froze me in place.

# chapter eighteen

# Run!

Run!

That was the only thought in my head.

Run!

But the gate was closed, and Mr. Tominski stood in front of it.

This was the first time I had seen him up close. He was a solid man. I noticed for the first time the size of his hands, his feet in their heavy black boots. They seemed to belong to a bigger man.

I was still on my knees in front of Anita's grave. The sun was beating down on my head, and Mr. Tominski with his huge hands stood between me and safety.

I managed to get to my feet and brush off my skirt. Grandmama had found out from Papa that Mr. Tominski didn't speak any English, only Polish, but he understood everything that was said.

"I b-better go," I said.

He did not move.

"M-Mama's expecting me."

He did not move.

"I was just taking a photograph."

He did not move.

"Grandmama gave me this camera."

Now he did move. With one huge hand he pointed to himself.

I thought for a moment he was trying to show me his suspenders, for they were brightly colored and stood out against his gray shirt.

He pointed again, jabbing his chest with intensity.

At that moment, I had the most startling thought. Mr. Tominski wanted to pose for a photograph. Mr. Tominski! I tried to keep the shock out of my voice as I said, "Would you like me to take a picture of you, Mr. Tominski?"

He nodded.

"Maybe you could sit on the bench."

I indicated the bench, and he took a seat. He ran one hand through his straggly hair, as if to smooth it, then rested his huge hands on his knees.

I approached the bench slowly. Of course he did

not eat children, as the Bellas had said. He was, as Mama had said, harmless. Yet, my heart pounded in my throat.

I looked through the viewfinder. Mr. Tominski had a serious look on his face, as if this was a big moment in his life. He took a deep breath, as if to inflate himself with importance, and held it.

"One . . . two . . . three."

I snapped the shutter. Mr. Tominski threw back his head and shouted with glee, "Hee! Hee! Hee!"

Then he grew quiet, but he continued to sit there, as if he were waiting.

My thoughts raced. Maybe, when Mr. Tominski was a boy back in the old country, he had seen important people having their pictures taken. Maybe he had promised himself that one day he would be important enough to have his picture made too.

And maybe, back then, if a person was very important, his picture would be taken twice, to make sure of a good one.

"Let me take one more," I said.

I looked through the viewfinder and saw his face

beaming with pride. "One . . . two . . . three." I took the picture.

Even as I clicked the shutter, I knew that I would need no photograph to help me remember this face. There was a glow about it. A radiance. A lambency!

When I looked up, the cemetery gate was open and Mr. Tominski was gone.

Not until I was around the house, listening to Lamar still trying to extract a promise from Abigail for a photograph, did my breathing return to normal.

That night at the dinner table, Grandmama said, "Girls, I want to know the most interesting thing you photographed today. One by one, now."

The Bellas had each photographed one of the spaniel puppies. Abigail admitted, blushing, that she had taken a picture of Lamar.

"A picture!" Augusta said.

"Augusta, what was your favorite photograph?" Grandmama interrupted quickly.

Augusta claimed that she could never take a picture of anything more wonderful than Adam.

"And you, Amie? You've been awfully quiet. What did you photograph today?"

"I photographed four things—Scout, Adam, a butterfly on the stone lamb of Anita's grave, and"—I was pleased that my voice didn't tremble when I said this—"I photographed Mr. Tominski."

Then I smiled at Papa. "There was a sort of lambency about him."

# chapter nineteen

# S-S-S-Something

"Scout! Where's Scout?" one of the Bellas said. "Scout likes to play. Scout!"

"Scout! Scooout!"

Both the Bellas called, but Scout did not appear. This was unusual. Scout always came when he was called.

"We'll have to play without him."

The Bellas and I were in the front yard getting ready to play Ain't No Bears Out Tonight.

For the first time, the Bellas were allowing me to be the bear. I was planning to hide in the shrubbery beneath the window to Papa's den. The Bellas hid their eyes and I rushed around the house and into the shrubbery.

I waited, heart pounding, not making a sound. I heard a noise behind me—faint and yet there was something urgent about it. I pulled aside the branches and looked down.

83

Scout lay on the ground. There was a broad black mark on his side that looked like blood. The faint sound, I saw now, came from his lungs attempting to get air.

His eyes rolled toward me and his tail gave one pitiful thump, as if apologizing for letting me see him like this.

I pushed through the bushes, ran past the Bellas and up the steps to the porch where Grandmama sat fanning herself in one of the chairs.

"S-S-S-S—"

I could not speak the word. I buried my face in Grandmama's skirt.

"S-S-S—"

"What is it?" Grandmama put one hand on my shoulder. "What's happened?"

When I still could not speak, she said, "Is it something the Bellas did? Where are the Bellas?

"Bellas! Bellas!" Instantly she was at the porch rail calling. "Girls!"

Augusta and Abigail came out of the house. "What's wrong?" Augusta asked

One of the Bellas said defensively, "Don't look at us. We didn't do anything. We were just playing a game."

"What game?"

"Ain't No Bears Out Tonight."

"Is that what scared you, Amie, the bear?"

"Grandmama, she *was* the bear. She begged to be the bear. We said she wouldn't be any good, but she—"

"Is that what scared you, Amie, being the bear?"

I shook my head and got out one word.

"S-S-Scout."

"The dog? Why, Scout's nothing to be afraid of. You love Scout."

"S-S-Scout's hurt. He can hardly breathe."

"Where?"

I pointed the way. Grandmama moved quickly, and we followed. She drew the branches aside and we peered around her.

Scout had not moved, except that his eyes no longer shifted to us, and his tail seemed to have lost its wag.

"Go in the house, girls."

"But, Grandmama—"

"Now."

As Abigail, Augusta, and I started for the house, Grandmama rapped on Papa's window. "Albert, I need you out here," she called. The tone of her voice made Papa move quickly. We passed him on the porch, and then went and sat on the stairs, shoulders touching for company.

"You get in the house too," Papa said, and the Bellas joined us.

"Scout's going to die," one of the Bellas said.

"If he does die, whoever did it will be sorry," said the other.

"Hush up!" Augusta said.

Papa came in. "Scout's going to die, isn't he?" a Bella asked.

"Go upstairs, girls."

We went upstairs and sat in the playroom. Nobody—not even the Bellas—felt like playing.

A short time later we heard a shot, and, as if that were the signal, we all burst into tears. Finally, Grandmama came up and told us Mama wanted to see us.

The last time I had been in Mama's room was when Adam was born. We now trailed in, a miserable group. Mama held out her hands. Abigail and Augusta managed to get there first, so the Bellas and I just stood by the bed.

Unbidden I thought of a poem.

*With five children to reach*
*Have a hand for each.*

I knew I would never write it down because it might make Mama unhappy not to have had enough hands to go around.

Our faces, reflected in the mirror over Mama's dressing table, were wet with tears. Mama began dusting them away with a small handkerchief.

"Scout wouldn't want you to be unhappy. Scout wouldn't want you to cry."

"What happened to him?" one of the Bellas asked.

"Yes," the other said. "We want to know what happened."

"Papa said maybe he got kicked by one of the horses," Mama explained.

"It couldn't have been a horse. Scout never bothered the horses," a Bella said. "He used to go for rides with us and he never once got near the horses."

"The horses liked him, Mama," added the other Bella.

"Sit down, girls." She patted the bed. We had

never been allowed to sit on Mama's bed before, so it didn't really feel comfortable.

She began to tell us stories about Scout, but I couldn't concentrate on anything but the way Scout had looked when I found him in the shrubbery.

"Now," Mama said, "have one little peep at your brother and then go downstairs. Cook has lemonade and cookies for you."

The Bellas and I left the room. Abigail and Augusta stayed behind for a longer look at Adam.

I expected the Bellas to rush down the stairs to the kitchen for the treat, but when we got out in the hall, the Bellas surprised me with one of their statements in unison.

"We know what happened."

"To Scout?"

"Yes, we know what happened."

"What?"

"He was killed!"

"No."

"Yes, somebody killed him—" and then they finished in unison "—and we know who!"

# chapter twenty

# Tominski!

"Tominski!" they cried together.

"Mr. Tominski?" I asked. "No. He wouldn't kill anybody. I think he's like Mama said—harmless."

"Well, I wouldn't call that harmless—killing our dog."

"*Murdering* our dog," the other Bella added.

Their tears were gone and their eyes had gotten little and mean.

"I really don't think he would have done such a terrible thing," I said.

I recalled the man with his doves, the gentle man who had inflated himself for a photograph and grinned with pleasure.

"What do you know?" a Bella sneered. "Go write a po-em."

"Yes, go write a po-em."

"Listen," I said, "I went back there one time, back

89

behind the chapel with Grandmama and Abigail. I didn't tell you because I was afraid you'd make me take you—"

"Take us!" a Bella exclaimed. "Why would we want you to take us? We've been there hundreds of times."

"Thousands," the other Bella said, correcting her twin for the first time in their lives.

"And one time—this is how we know he killed Scout—and one time Scout followed us, and when Mr. Tominski got his doves flying around his head, Scout came running into the clearing and Mr. Tominski kicked him. He missed the first time, but he was getting ready to kick him again—"

The second Bella picked up the tale—"when we rushed out and kicked *him*, and he ran into the woods and took his doves with him."

I knew the Bellas well, and I could tell when they made things up. This had the ring of truth.

"But, but just because he tried to kick him once, doesn't mean he killed him. Mama said she thought it was a horse."

"Didn't you see the black mark on Scout's side?"

"Yes, it was blood."

"Not just blood. There was a black streak."

"And black streaks like that don't come from a horse."

"They come from a boot."

As they said this, I was back in the cemetery, taking a photograph of Mr. Tominski. I recalled his big feet, his black boots.

"Tominski's boots."

"Remember when you and Abigail and Augusta went around the house with Grandmama?"

"Yes."

"Well, we didn't. We went in the bushes and looked at Scout, and his ribs had been kicked in."

"Here's what happened. Scout went back to look at the doves and old man Tominski saw him and kicked him."

"Yes, he kicked him so hard that Scout fell over."

They were taking turns, sharing the miserable story, and I turned from one twin to the other, listening.

"He might even have kicked him twice. We couldn't turn Scout over to look at the other side."

"And then Scout crawled to the house. He crawled to Papa, but the closest he could get was the window to Papa's study."

"Yes, then he lay down."

It all sounded as if it might have happened that way.

"But you can't be sure," I said. For some reason I didn't want it to be Mr. Tominski's fault.

"We are sure. And old man Tominski is going to pay for killing our dog."

"Girls," Mama called from her room, "what's the trouble?"

"Nothing, Mama," the Bellas lied together.

"Then go downstairs and have your lemonade."

"Yes, Mama."

As we went downstairs, I glanced at the Bellas, and I could tell from the looks on their faces that they meant what they said.

Grandmama joined us in the kitchen, something she had never done before, and I thought Mama must have sent her.

She took in our solemn faces, our uneaten cookies, our untasted lemonade. She said, "It's perfectly all right to grieve for a pet. When I was a girl, I myself cried when my pony Bonny Bill died."

"What did he die of?" a Bella asked.

"He ate some poison berries."

"Did someone give them to him?"

"He found them quite on his own."

"He could have been poisoned."

"He could have been murdered like Scout."

Grandmama ignored the twins' last remarks. "As I said, it's perfectly all right to grieve for a pet, but you can't go back. You need to dry your tears and turn your faces to the future."

# chapter twenty-one

# Uncle William
# and the Dog Star

"Uncle William! It's Uncle William!"

The five of us ran down the steps to greet our favorite uncle. Actually he was our only uncle, but if we had had a dozen, he would have been our favorite.

It had been only one month since we had run down these same steps to greet Grandmama. One month and so much had happened. Not only had I gotten a new brother, but I had also learned the depth of my feeling for him. Not only had I lost a beloved dog, but I had also been there for the last sad wag of his tail.

Only one month ago, Mama had called us her white butterflies, and although I flitted across the lawn in the same white pinafore with my sisters, the description no longer seemed to fit me.

"My favorite nieces," Uncle William cried. The Bellas got there first, and he swung them into the air. "*Mia bella* Bellas," he said, pretending to be Italian. Then, "Abigail, the fair! Augusta, the dear! And Amen, the answer to an uncle's prayer!" My embrace was the last.

He greeted each of us in a special way, and although Abigail and Augusta were too old to be twirled in the air, I was glad I was not.

Grandmama stood on the porch, smiling. "My favorite son," she said and kissed him.

The reason for Uncle William's visit was to see his new nephew, but I was especially glad to see him because perhaps he was the one person who could soften the loss of our dog, and make the Bellas forget their sworn revenge.

Uncle William went upstairs first to visit Mama, and after he had admired Adam and we had eaten supper, he did what he was famous for—told us stories.

My uncle was a wonderful storyteller. His stories were of the heavens. He loved the stars, the moon, the planets. He yearned to solve their mysteries.

As we sat at his feet that night, he told of going to the Yerkes Observatory. "Girls, there is a moving floor. It rises." As he told of the rising floor, he rose from his chair, looking around in amazement, as if our library floor were doing the same thing. "It lifted me to the eyepiece, where I saw miracles—the craters of the moon, the satellites of Jupiter, the spectacular rings of Saturn."

He told of a man named Tesla. "Remember, Mother, he was the man I saw at the world's fair holding lights—electric lights, girls, wireless electric lights, one in each hand." He was such an actor that as he stood with his hands outstretched, they seemed to glow.

"There was an article in *Electrical World* called 'Is Tesla to Signal the Stars?' The man's going to contact life on Mars!"

"Papa, could that be?" Augusta asked. "Could there be life on Mars?"

"Your uncle is telling the story," Papa said shortly. He loved Mama but seemed to suffer the rest of her family.

It was one of the Bellas who interrupted to ask, "Isn't there a *dog* star, Uncle William?" She emphasized the word *dog*, and I knew, if the adults didn't, that she was turning the conversation to Scout.

"I'll draw it," Uncle William said with enthusiasm. He rose at once and went to Papa's desk. We, pulled along in the wake of his enthusiasm, followed.

We bent over his shoulder and watched as he drew from memory tiny stars and then connected them to form the outline of the dog. "This is Sirius," he said, going over the star with the tip of his pen. "Sirius is the brightest star and it is the dog tag, here at the throat."

"Speaking of dogs," one of the Bellas said with studied casualness, "did you hear what happened to our dog Scout?"

Mama's hand touched her forehead when she heard the tone of the Bella's voice, and she now rose. "Bedtime! Pauline, the children need to go to bed."

"Mama, I'm not finished," Bella said. "I was in the middle of saying something to Uncle William."

"Bedtime," Aunt Pauline said.

"Mama, you always said we shouldn't interrupt people," the other Bella complained.

"Uncle William will be here tomorrow to answer all your questions," Mama said.

"And tomorrow night," Uncle William said, "we'll lie outside and I'll show you Polaris and Orion and Venus."

"And Sirius?" a Bella said with a glance at Mama.

"Yes, Sirius too."

Quickly Aunt Pauline herded us toward the stairs before there could be any more talk of dog stars.

But I knew that the Bellas' minds, fueling each other, would soon return to their topic of interest— the death, no, the murder of our dog Scout.

I heard Mama say to Uncle William, "Don't encourage the Bellas to talk about Scout."

"I didn't! I was talking about Sirius!"

"I know, but the Bellas have a one-track mind these days. They're determined to talk about what they think happened to Scout."

"Oh, William," Grandmama said, changing the subject, "when are you ever going to come down to earth?"

"As long as there are stars, dear mother, never!" Uncle William replied.

# chapter twenty-two

# Venus and Mars

"Venus...Orion...Capella..."

We were on our backs, staring up at the starlit sky. The house was dark so that we would not be distracted by other lights.

The night air was clean and clear, and the stars seemed unusually close. I had never before been able to see the constellations, but now the sky seemed full of figures and motion.

There was Orion with his sparkling belt and shield. The Bull's horns stretched across the sky. The Archer flexed his bow. The Charioteer drove his team. The Herdsman played his pipe.

And the words, the words were among the most beautiful I had ever heard. You could make up a whole poem out of nothing but stars and constellations.

Aquarius...Pegasus...the Lyre...the Lion... Mercury...Mars.

One of the twins interrupted my thoughts. "And where is the Dog Star?"

Her voice was studiedly innocent. Uncle William had apparently forgotten that dogs were not to be mentioned.

"There is the dog. Sirius is the dog tag." Uncle William pointed.

Papa had been with us, leaning against one of the willows, but he had gone into the house for his pipe, so the Bellas were taking the opportunity to bring the conversation around to Scout.

"Did you hear what happened to our dog, Uncle William?"

Now Uncle William brought his thoughts down to earth. He must have remembered Mama's warning because he switched the conversation to another topic.

"Oh, the twins," he cried with enthusiasm. "You two will want to see the twins—Castor and Pollux. Pollux is the brightest."

"Mr. Tominski killed our dog!"

"Yes, Mr. Tominski killed our dog!" the other Bella echoed.

Her voice was loud enough to carry into the

house. Papa quickly appeared on the porch, but it was too late.

"Mr. Tominski killed Scout. He kicked him. We saw the black marks from his boot on Scout's side. Mr. Tominski is a murderer!"

"Oh, hush," Abigail said. "We're trying to learn something about the stars."

"Mr. Tominski is a murderer!" the Bellas said together.

A light came on upstairs in Mama's room. And in the square of light that fell across the bushes, I saw something move.

A figure slipped around the edge of the light, but I saw the bright suspenders against the darker shirt.

Mr. Tominski had been on the edge of the family, enjoying the stars with us. He must have heard the Bellas' terrible words: "Mr. Tominski is a murderer!"

Papa came around the porch on the run. "That is enough, Bellas," he said as he joined us.

"But, Papa—"

"If you aren't going to learn about the stars, go into the house."

My eyes searched the shadows for Mr. Tominski, but he was gone.

"You must not have loved Scout at all," one of the Bellas accused, made bold by the darkness.

"Enough!"

The word rang out with such force that even the crickets seemed to fall silent.

"Albert," Mama called from her window. "Is everything all right?"

"Yes, Lily."

The light went out in Mama's bedroom. In the hush that followed, Papa said in a more reasonable voice, "I loved the dog very much, but there will be other dogs. There may not be another clear night to enjoy the stars during Uncle William's visit."

There was another silence, and I thought I heard a twig snap in the orchard.

I glanced quickly at Papa, but apparently I was the only one aware that Mr. Tominski was making his way home.

# chapter twenty-three

# What Was Wrong

"What is it, Birdie?"

"Gentleman to see you, sir."

Papa frowned. We were having our evening meal in the dining room and Papa did not allow interruptions. Also this was the first time that Mama had felt like joining us for supper since Adam's birth, and Papa wanted it to be special.

Uncle William had been in the middle of an explanation of what we had seen last night. "And if it's clear tonight, I'll show you—"

In the mirror over the buffet I could see the other side of Papa's face, which looked somehow even more displeased.

"It's the sheriff, sir," Birdie explained, twisting her apron in her distress. "He says it's important."

Papa got up at once, crumpled his napkin, and laid it beside his plate. He left the room and closed the door behind him. We fell silent but could hear nothing.

Grandmama said, "There's probably trouble at the lumber mill."

"The mill doesn't operate at night, Grandmama," Abigail said.

Grandmama silenced her with a look. "Then at the bank," she said. "I do believe bank robbers operate day and night."

No one seemed to have any more suggestions. Even the Bellas were quiet—awed, perhaps, as I was by the fact that Sheriff Walkins was in our front hall.

The sheriff had never been to our home before, but I had seen him in town. He was a big cold-eyed man, whose size alone could have kept law and order. His entrance into The Willows seemed to bring a chill that touched even our candlelit dining room.

Mama appeared frozen, her hands stiff on either side of her plate.

Papa was gone for some time. When he returned, his face was pale. His mouth was set. A muscle worked in his jaw.

"What is it, Albert?" Mama said.

He had to force the two words out. "Mr. Tom."

"The dove keeper?" Grandmama said, puzzled, as if he were the last person she had considered.

Papa nodded and cleared his throat. "It seems he was trying to hop a train. At least that's what the sheriff thinks."

"Hop a train? But why? Where would he go?" Mama asked.

Papa lifted his shoulders and let them drop.

"And *hop* a train? If he had come to you, Albert, you would have bought him a ticket," she continued in her reasonable voice. "There was no need to leave like…"

She trailed off and Aunt Pauline finished it with "—like a thief in the night. I always said—"

"Be quiet," Papa said to her in the sternest voice I had ever heard him use with his sister.

"What happened, Albert?" Grandmama asked.

"The fireman on the train said Mr. Tom was just standing by the tracks as he often did. The fireman blew the whistle in greeting. He didn't even know there'd been an accident till he reached the station."

Mama looked at Papa, as if she were having a hard time understanding. "An accident, Albert?"

Papa nodded.

"Mr. Tom is injured?" Now she got up purposefully. "You must bring him here to the house. Birdie!"

Birdie was still standing in the doorway to the kitchen, her apron twisted out of recognition.

Papa shook his head. "It's too late."

"Dead?" Mama sank back into her chair. "Oh, no. No!"

Papa said nothing.

"I'm trying to remember the last time I saw him alive," Mama said.

I didn't have to try to remember. I had seen him last night turning away from those hurtful words, *Mr. Tominski is a murderer!* a shadow in the moonlight, going home. I thought he had been heading toward his doves, but now I knew he had been heading away from us forever.

Aunt Pauline broke the silence. She said, "I trust you all remember that I dreamed of a graveyard. I knew someone would die. I'm just glad it wasn't one of—"

"Pauline, please!" Mama said.

"—us!"

Papa sighed. "The sheriff's waiting for me. I'm going into town. I don't know when I'll be home."

Uncle William rose. "I'll go with you, Albert."

"I'd be grateful for your company," Papa said.

He crossed the room, kissed Mama's cheek, and then he and Uncle William departed.

I glanced across the table to where the Bellas sat, side by side. They seemed deflated. Their faces showed none of the satisfaction I had expected, instead a sort of disappointment, as if they had been cheated of their revenge. Perhaps they felt they had had no active part in a train accident.

I would not be the one to tell them that they had.

# chapter twenty-four

# *X* Marks the Spot

*X* marks the spot.

I lay in bed, overcome with an emotion I could not name. There was probably a word for the way I felt, but feelings were the hardest things to find a word for.

As I lay there, The Willows took the form of a giant map, covered with Xs.

*X*—the spot where Mr. Tom got off the train years ago.

*X*—where he found my wounded father and carried him to safety.

*X*—his home in the chapel where he lived for twenty-five years.

*X*—the stump where he sat, laughing, while the doves flew over his head.

*X*—the bench in the cemetery, where he sat grinning his gap-toothed smile, and I took his photograph.

*X*—where my sisters and I lay under the stars and Mr. Tom heard himself called a murderer.

And the final *X*—his grave, where we had his funeral this afternoon.

"Surely, *surely*," Aunt Pauline had said, "you are not going to bury him in the family cemetery!"

Papa said, "I am."

"But that is for family."

"Mr. Tom is family. Those were our father's exact words. 'Mr. Tom is family.' Our father didn't say, 'Mr. Tom is like family.'"

"I never heard Father say that. And I, for one, could not rest easy in my grave, knowing that that man lay in the same sacred place."

"Then I am sorry to tell you, dear sister, that you will not rest easy," Papa said.

It was Papa who led the brief ceremony. He wore his white linen suit. He held his hands behind his back, the fingers so tightly clasped that his knuckles were whiter than his suit. His head was bowed.

Aunt Pauline and Mama sat on the bench. Aunt Pauline was stern and indignant. Mama was tearful, but I thought perhaps her tears were not so much for

Mr. Tominski as for her suffering and inconsolable husband.

The Bellas did not attend. Grandmama and Uncle William had taken them into town.

Abigail and Augusta began the service with a song, for once in perfect harmony.

> *"Just as I am, without one plea*
> *But that Thy blood was shed for me,*
> *And that Thou bidst me come to Thee,*
> *O Lamb of God, I come, I come."*

My thoughts drifted back to the last time I had heard my sisters sing, the time I had seen Mr. Tominski's smiling face at the window. I was saddened by the thought of my needless fears.

"Greater love," Papa began, "hath no man than this, that he lay down his life for his friend."

Papa then spoke about how Mr. Tom, a fugitive from justice, had risked capture to save him. This was the first time I had heard Mr. Tom was a fugitive, and I was still wondering about that when Papa said, "I believe Amie has a poem she would like to read."

I unrolled my sheet of paper. The air around me

seemed changed, hard to breath. At that moment we heard the mournful sound of the train. Ever since Mr. Tominski's accident, the engineer had been blowing his whistle from twenty miles away, clearing the tracks, trying to prevent another tragedy.

I took a deep breath. All the graves bore flowers for the occasion, but on this sad day even the flowers seemed to scent the air with unhappiness.

"Amie," Papa prompted.

I read.

> *"He came to us on the noonday train.*
> *The train that took him away again.*
> *He was a gentle man, his loves*
> *Were our family and his doves.*
> *A shy and simple man and yet*
> *He touched us and we'll not forget.*
> *I think Grandmama said it best:*
> *The dove magician's gone to rest."*

Papa nodded to Abigail and Augusta, and they began a final hymn.

> *"Blest be the tie that binds*
> *Our hearts in Christian love!*

*The fellowship of kindred minds*
*Is like to that above."*

Papa began to weep. He put his hands over his face and his shoulders shook.

So, I thought, there are two times in a man's life when he cries—when he gains a son and when he loses a friend.

The last verse brought tears to all our eyes.

*"When we asunder part*
*It gives us inward pain;*
*But we shall still be joined in heart,*
*And hope to meet again."*

When the song ended, the women and children went back into the house. We moved through the empty rooms in silence, listening to the clumps of earth being shoveled into Mr. Tominski's grave.

# chapter twenty-five

# No Longer Young

"Your poem was fine, Amie."

"I wish it could have been better."

"It was fine."

"Papa, I've been thinking about what you said at the funeral. Can I ask you a question?"

"You ask too many questions, Amie."

"How else can I learn, Papa?"

We were back behind the chapel, where the doves cooed in their cages. The way the limbs of the trees arched over our heads made it seem like an outdoor chapel. Behind us, Mr. Tom's chapel had been closed, the door and windows nailed shut.

"At the funeral you said Mr. Tom was a fugitive."

"Yes."

"A fugitive from what?"

"I don't mind telling you now, Amen, but I wouldn't want it to go any further."

"It won't."

"Well, like a lot of young Polish immigrants, Mr. Tom came to this country to work in the Kentucky coal mines. There was a murder—I don't know the details—but Mr. Tom was the lead suspect. He escaped before he could be arrested."

"Did the police come after him?"

"They didn't track him to The Willows, if that's what you mean, but all his life he was afraid they would. He would never go into town. He hid from visitors. He relied on me for everything."

Papa put his hands in his pockets and looked up at the sky. "I think that night when, as you told me, he must have heard the twins call him a murderer, all he could think of was what had happened in Kentucky."

"And he was afraid all over again."

"He was a very simple man, Amen, and his mind in many ways was like a child's."

"Do you think he did kill Scout?"

"Maybe he kicked the dog. I don't know. The night he escaped, there were dogs after him, tracking him, and I don't think he had much love for dogs after that."

"Anyway, Papa, I'm very, very glad he saved your life."

"I am too, Amie."

After a minute I said, "So that's another thing he was—a fugitive. How many things can one man be? Aunt Pauline said he was a drifter, a hobo. Mama called him a harmless old man. Grandmama called him a dove magician. You said he was a friend. I think he was a hero for saving your life. Can a man be so many things?"

"So many things—and more."

He stepped back to the dove cage and opened it. The doves flew out and landed in the trees. They waited, their heads cocked to one side. I think they hoped that Mr. Tominski would come out and call them into action.

"He's not coming," Papa said to the doves. "Go back to the woods." He made a shooing motion with both hands.

"Will they be all right, Papa?"

"Mr. Tom got them from the woods. He made little traps and brought them here. Now they're just going home."

We waited for a while, watching the doves' confusion, and then one of them flew to a nearby tree. Another followed.

"You know what I was going to do that day, the day Mr. Tom saved my life?"

"No, Papa."

"I was going dove hunting." Both of us smiled at the thought.

When all the doves had disappeared in the forest, Papa brushed his hands together.

He said, "Well, it's all over now." And, taking my hand, he started toward home.

A shadow fell across our path as a cloud hid the sun. I thought it was a warning that a storm was coming. I looked up. The rest of the sky was blue. Our storm had come and gone.

I said, "Papa, somehow I don't feel as young as I felt a few days ago."

"Nor do I," said Papa. "Nor do I."

# chapter twenty-six

# Z Is Not the End

"*Zzzzzzzzz.* Hear that, Adam? That means there is a bee inside that flower. Listen."

*Zzzzzzzzzzz.*

"When you hear *zzzzz,* Adam, you don't pick that flower. You don't even smell that flower."

I held Adam's small hand as we watched the flower, waiting for the bee to exit.

It had been two years since Mr. Tominski's funeral. Many things had happened in that two years. We had moved into a new century. The Willows now had electricity, and Papa was talking of a motor car.

The Bellas had gone to live with Grandmama, where they attended something called Miss Bridges Finishing School, though the few times they had been home, Papa said they didn't seem quite finished.

Abigail would be marrying Lamar in the fall. All the sisters would be in the wedding. We already had our dresses—peach organza with embroidered sashes. Aunt Pauline said she didn't think she could attend, because her wedding to Frederick would have been in the fall. However, she had her dress made just in case.

"Here he comes, Adam. Bee!"

Adam said, "McBee."

"No, you're a McBee." I touched his shoulder. "That is a bee."

Adam was two years old now. I had taken over his education, the way the Bellas had taken over mine.

"Listen, Adam, do you hear any more *zzzzzz*?"

Adam put his small hand behind his ear. That was what Aunt Pauline did when there was something she wanted to hear. Adam shook his head.

"Then we can pick that flower."

I picked it and added it to the others in the crook of my arm.

"Two years ago, Adam, there was a man who lived here—a dove keeper. And I never really got to know him. He went away too soon."

"On the choo-choo train?"

That was too painful a question to answer.

"But one time—right in this very cemetery—for one brief moment, I had the strange feeling that I did know him. Anyway, today we're going to put some flowers on his grave."

"Let's go," he said, his favorite phrase.

We opened the angel gate to the cemetery and stepped inside. Mr. Tominski's grave now had a tombstone.

*Mr. Anton Tominski*
*Keeper of the Doves*
*Departed this day, August 11, 1899*

"Lamb," Adam said, running to Anita's grave to pat its head.

He continued proudly, "Ear . . . eye . . . nose . . ."

He looked to me for praise. My eyes had misted over because I remembered that day long ago when I recited all the parts of our dog, Scout.

"Good, Adam."

". . . tail . . ." he continued.

I laid the roses in front of the stone. Then, with a sigh, I crossed to where Adam knelt beside the lamb. I looked at Anita's inscription.

Someday, I said to myself, someday I will write about you, Anita, because even though you only lived ten days, you seemed to make each day count for the people who loved you. You held your sisters' hands, you smiled, you were loved. You're still loved. You never, ever cried.

I lifted my head with a sudden thought. And maybe, Mr. Tominski, one day I'll write about you.

"You know, Adam," I said aloud, "there are poems, there are stories, whole books, about people who lived hundreds, even thousands of years ago. Those people still live because of words. Words! Words are the most wonderful things in the world. As long as there are words, nobody need ever die."

"Let's go," Adam said.

"Let's."

And as I closed the gate behind us and the latch clicked shut, I somehow seemed to be closing more than just a gate.

"I like the lamb," Adam said.

"And you knew the words for all the parts."

"Yes."

"You are a smart boy."

"Yes!"

We started for the house. Adam looked back once for a final glimpse of the lamb while I, as Grandmama would say, turned my face to the future.

## Other Books by Betsy Byars